Katie AND THE STARRY NIGHT

JAMES MAYHEW

ORCHARD

For
Rebecca, Paco & Marco
and for Marlene
with love,
J. M.

With sincere thanks to everyone at Orchard Books, especially my editor, Liz, and my designer, Clare.
Thanks also to Gabriel and the Brown family for helping with the endpapers.

ORCHARD BOOKS
338 Euston Road, London NW1 3BH
Orchard Books Australia
Level 17/207 Kent Street, Sydney, NSW 2000

ISBN 978 1 40833 243 6

First published in 2012 by Orchard Books
First published in paperback in 2013
This edition published in 2015

Text and illustrations © James Mayhew 2012/2015

The rights of James Mayhew to be identified as the author and
illustrator of this work have been asserted by him in accordance
with the Copyright, Designs and Patents Act, 1988.
A CIP catalogue record for this book is available from the British Library.

2 4 6 8 10 9 7 5 3 1

Printed in China

Orchard Books is a division of Hachette Children's Books,
an Hachette UK company.
www.hachette.co.uk

www.jamesmayhew.co.uk

Acknowledgements
The Starry Night, June 1889 (oil on canvas), Gogh, Vincent van (1853-90) / Museum of Modern Art, New York, USA /
Bridgeman Images. *Vincent's Chair*, 1888 (oil on canvas), Gogh, Vincent van (1853-90) / National Gallery, London, UK /
Bridgeman Images. *Noon, or The Siesta, after Millet*, 1890 (oil on canvas), Gogh, Vincent van (1853-90) / Musee d'Orsay,
Paris, France / Bridgeman Images. *The Olive Orchard*, 1889 (oil on canvas), Gogh, Vincent van (1853-90) / National
Gallery of Art, Washington DC, USA / Bridgeman Images. *Fishing Boats on the Beach at Saintes-Maries-de-la-Mer* (oil on
canvas), Gogh, Vincent van (1853-90) / Van Gogh Museum, Amsterdam, The Netherlands / Bridgeman Images.

KATIE AND GRANDMA loved to go on trips together. Sometimes, for a treat, Grandma took Katie to the art gallery.

One day, they went to see some paintings
by Vincent van Gogh. Katie's favourite was
called *The Starry Night*.
"It looks magical," she said. "Like a dream."
"Talking of dreams," said Grandma,
"I could do with a nap."

Royal borough of Greenwich
Eltham Library

Checkout summary

**Name: Miss Sreebhadra
Punchepady Jibin**
Date: 20/05/2024 09:25

Loaned today

Title: Florence Nightingale
ID: 38028024726199
Due back: 10/06/2024

Title: Superpowered animals : meet the
world's strongest, smartest and
swiftest cre
ID: 38028025429553
Due back: 10/06/2024

Total item(s) loaned today : 2
Previous Amount Owed: 0.00 GBP
Overdue : 0
Reservation(s) pending: 0
Reservation(s) to collect: 0
Total item(s) on loan 2

For renewals and information
Tel 01527 852384 (24 hr)
www.better.org.uk/greenwichlibraries

Katie looked more closely at the picture.
The stars seemed to be moving. Grandma was
almost asleep, so Katie quietly climbed through
the picture frame and into the painting . . .

The dazzling stars sparkled and swirled.
They looked close enough to touch,
so Katie reached out . . . and grasped one!
"I must show Grandma," she said,
putting the star safely in her pocket.

Jumping back into the gallery, Katie saw some other stars twirling after her.

"Perhaps they want to play!" she laughed, jumping up to catch them. But she couldn't quite reach.

"Hmm, I need something to stand on," said Katie.
She saw a picture called *Vincent's Chair*.
"That's perfect!" she smiled.

Katie quickly dragged the chair out of the picture,
as more and more stars tumbled into the gallery.

But, even standing on the chair, Katie couldn't reach all the stars, and some floated into another picture called *Noon*. She decided to chase after them and so climbed through the frame.

A young couple were napping in the shade on a hot summer's day. The stars tumbled into the sky, and night soon fell upon the countryside.

The woman, whose name was Marie, woke up.
"Oh, look at all the stars!" she said. "Surely they don't belong in this painting."
"Er . . . no," said Katie. "Would you help me catch them?"

Climbing up the haystack, Katie and Marie had a wonderful time jumping to catch the stars and landing in the soft hay.

But when they jumped back into the gallery,
the spinning stars slipped through their fingers
once again.

"We must get them back in their painting before
the gallery guard sees they're missing!" said Marie.

But even Marie wasn't tall enough
to catch them.
"Look, there's a ladder!" said Katie,
spotting a picture called *The Olive Grove*.
She quickly clambered through the frame.

Women were gathering olives from a tree.

"Please, can I borrow your ladder?" asked Katie.

"I have to catch some stars!"

The ladies laughed. "*Ma chérie*, you cannot
catch stars."

"You can, with a ladder," said Katie.

"Come and help me!"

They all raced back into the gallery, and the olive pickers held the ladder steady as Katie climbed up to catch the twirling stars. It was tricky work because the stars wouldn't keep still! The more Katie tried to catch them, the more they spun away.

The stars were drifting towards another
painting called *Fishing Boats on the Beach*.
"Come on! We must catch them!" said Marie.
They all climbed inside.

In the picture, the stars were caught
on a breeze and twirled out to sea.
"How will we reach them now?"
asked Marie.

"Let's take a boat," said Katie.
"Oh, yes! A boat ride!" said the
olive pickers, giggling.

They sailed across the sea as the stars sparkled in the sky.
"Oh, what shall we do?" worried Marie. "The stars are so high."
Katie saw a big fishing net in the boat. "Let's try this!" she said.

They all threw the net as high as they could . . . and caught the stars!
"At last!" said Katie, as everyone cheered.

Back in the gallery, they all quickly ran to
The Starry Night picture.
"Now, we can put the stars back before the
guard finds out," said Katie.

They threw the stars into the sky but it didn't look quite right.
"What's that in your pocket, Katie?" asked Marie.
"My star!" said Katie. "I wanted to show it to Grandma . . . "

"But it might float away again," said Marie. "Put it in *The Starry Night* and then you can see it whenever you want." So, Katie threw the star up into the painting.

"Thank you, everyone," said Katie.
"We did it!"

"And now we must return to our pictures, too,"
said Marie. "Au revoir, ma chérie."
"Goodbye!" called Katie.

Katie put the chair back where
it belonged, just in time, as the
gallery guard came past.
"Phew!" said Katie. "Hello."
"Good afternoon," he said.

And then Grandma woke up.
"Oh, I must have nodded off,"
she said. "I had a lovely dream
about stars."
Katie giggled.

That night, Katie and Grandma looked out of the window.

It was a beautiful starry night.

"The stars look almost alive," said Grandma.

"Perhaps they are," laughed Katie.

Grandma smiled. "Perhaps," she said. "Goodnight, Katie."

Vincent van Gogh loved to paint the stars.
Sometimes he painted outside at night. He put candles
on his hat so he could see what he was doing!

I like the way Van Gogh's stars twirl around, so I've
painted a twirly starry sky, too. Why don't you make a starry
sky like this? All you need to do is use colours like Van Gogh.
You can use paint or crayons, or even collage. Lots of blues
and purples for the sky, and yellows and oranges for the stars
and moon will soon help you create your own masterpiece!

Love Katie x